Hannah the Hamster Hunter

BY MARCIA LEONARD
PICTURES BY MAXIE CHAMBLISS

Grolier Enterprises Inc., Danbury, Connecticut

Note to Parents

On Hannah's first day of school, Speedy the classroom hamster disappeared from his cage. *How did that happen?* Did he grow wings and fly away . . . did he join the fish in the aquarium for a swim . . . did he escape through the open cage door . . . or did he turn into a boy and join the class?

Children get to decide what has caused various events to occur in this heartwarming story about Hannah's eventful first day of school. As you share the book with your child, you'll find questions about what happened to Hannah, along with four possible choices. Three of the choices are improbable; only one makes sense. Once your child chooses the right answer, you can continue reading the story.

With this multiple-choice design, HANNAH THE HAMSTER HUNTER will help children understand the process of cause and effect. Educators think that this skill is a key to success in school, because it teaches kids *how* to think. So you can give your child a learning head start by exploring the ideas in this book—and in all the other Good Thinking™ Club books.

Remember to make use of the question-and-answer format as you read the story aloud. Talk about what happens to Hannah, teach your child new words and concepts, spark laughter and discussion. Then explore other examples of cause and effect by asking, "How did *that* happen?" You're sure to find that this kind of learning is fun and rewarding—for both you and your child.

Produced by Small Packages, Inc.

Logo and cover design by Nancy Stevens Norton

Originally published by Silver Press, a division of Silver Burdette Press, Inc.
Simon & Schuster, Inc., Prentise Hall Bldg., Englewood Cliffs, NJ 07632

"Hurry up, Hannah!" Daddy called from downstairs.
"You don't want to be late on your first day of school."
Hannah hurried. She brushed her teeth in record time.
Then she raced downstairs to the front door,
where her daddy was waiting with baby Rose.

She picked up her new backpack and stepped outside. Halfway down the walk, she realized that her head and shoulders were wet!

Now how do you suppose that happened?

Did a giant sprinkle her
with his watering can?

Did a big cloud shower her
with raindrops?

Did an elephant water her
with its trunk?

Or did a speedboat splash her
as it went by?

"It's raining, it's pouring, the old man is snoring," sang Hannah. "Come on back into the house," said Daddy. "You'll need your rainboots and slicker."

By the time she finally reached school, Hannah *was* late.
The other kids in her class were already busy playing,
and she felt a little shy coming into the room alone.
Her teacher Miss Joyce seemed to understand.

She took Hannah by the hand and introduced her to some of the children. "Polly, Tom, Brandie—this is Hannah," she said. "Will you share the paints with her?" The children nodded, and soon Hannah was painting a picture of a clown. Then suddenly, purple spots spattered across her paper!

How do you think that happened?

Did she bump the
purple paint jar by accident?

Did she cry purple tears
onto her paper?

Did she drip grape jelly
from a sandwich?

Or did she drop purple petals
from a flower?

Everyone looked at Hannah's picture. "What happened?" asked Tom. "I bumped the paint jar," said Hannah. "Now my clown is ruined!" "I think we can fix your painting," said Miss Joyce. And she showed Hannah how to make the purple spots into polka dots on the clown's costume.

Hannah finished her painting. Then she and the other kids
decided to play circus with the dress-up clothes.
"I'll be a clown, like the one in my picture," said Hannah.
She put on a funny red hat and some big grown-up shoes.

Polly was an acrobat, Brandie was a lion tamer, and Tom was a lion. They had so much fun playing circus, they didn't notice what else was going on in the classroom. But finally Hannah looked around —and saw that the big table by the window was full of snacks!

How did that happen?

Did a wizard make them
appear by magic?

Did some ants carry them
in from a picnic?

Did a paperboy deliver them
on his bicycle?

Or did Miss Joyce set them
out for the children?

Miss Joyce finished setting out the snacks. There was apple juice, animal crackers, and green grapes. And Hannah enjoyed everything.

After that they sang songs and played a few games.
Then Miss Joyce introduced everyone to the class pets:
Speedy the hamster, who lived in a wire cage,
and some tropical fish, who lived in a big glass tank.

She let a few of the children hold Speedy. Then she put him back in his cage while she showed the class how to feed the fish. When she turned around, the cage was empty. Speedy was gone!

How did that happen?

Did Speedy grow wings
and fly away?

Did he join the fish for a swim?

Did he escape through
the open cage door?

Or did he turn into a boy
and join the class?

"Time for a hamster hunt, children," said Miss Joyce. "I must have left the cage door open, because Speedy has escaped." Everyone searched high and low. But there was no sign of Speedy. "Where would I go if *I* were a hamster?" thought Hannah. She looked for a place that was cozy and soft and just right for a nap.

And there was Speedy, taking a snooze in the funny red hat in the box of dress-up clothes! Gently she put him back in his cage. "Thank you, Hannah," said Miss Joyce. "You did such a fine job of hamster hunting, you may be pet monitor for a whole week."

By the time the morning was over, Hannah was happy but tired.
So much had happened on her first day of school!
"I wonder what will happen *tomorrow*," thought Hannah.
And she ran to meet her daddy and baby Rose.